Yum!

Written by Zoë Clarke
Illustrated by Sandra Aguilar

Collins

2

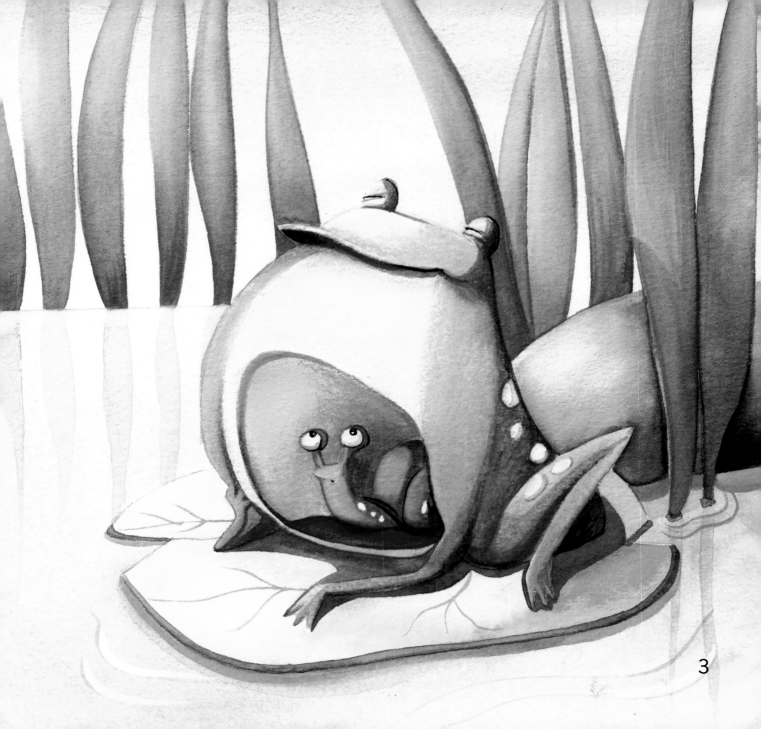

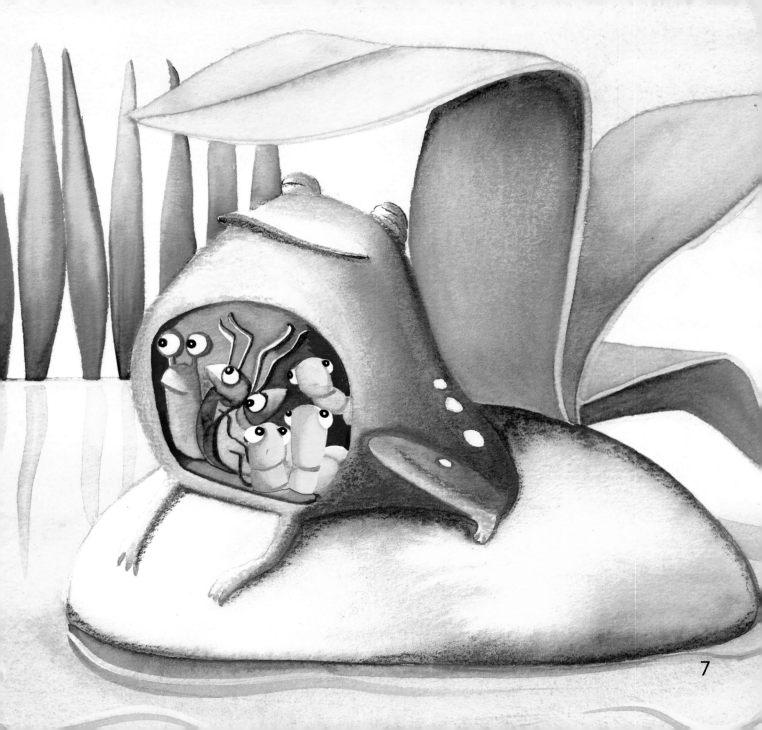

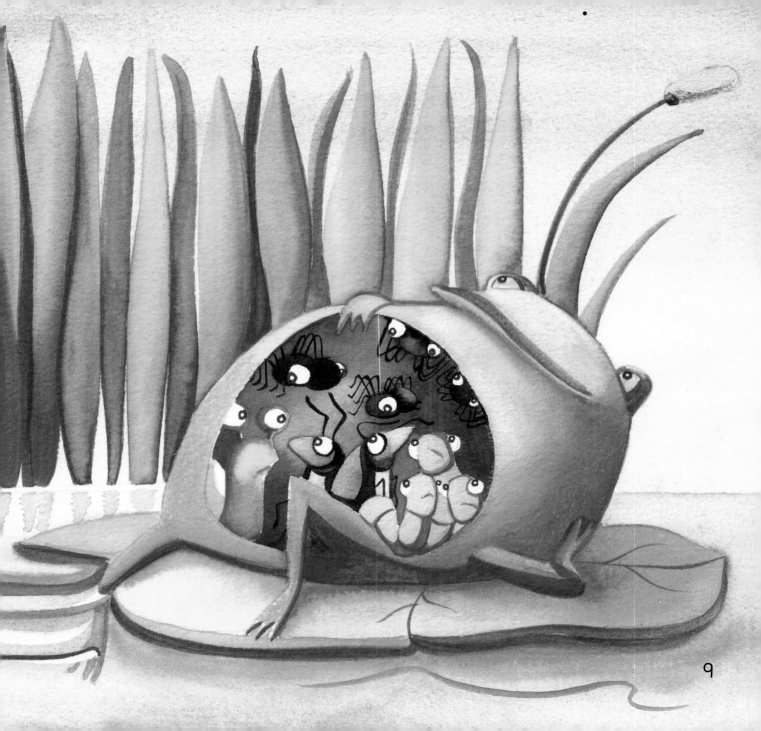

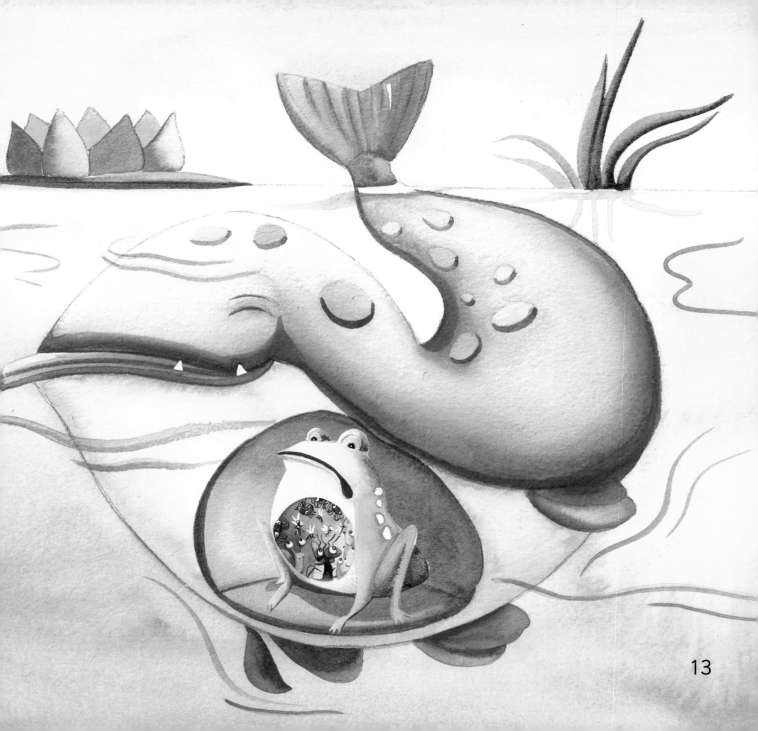

Yum, yum!

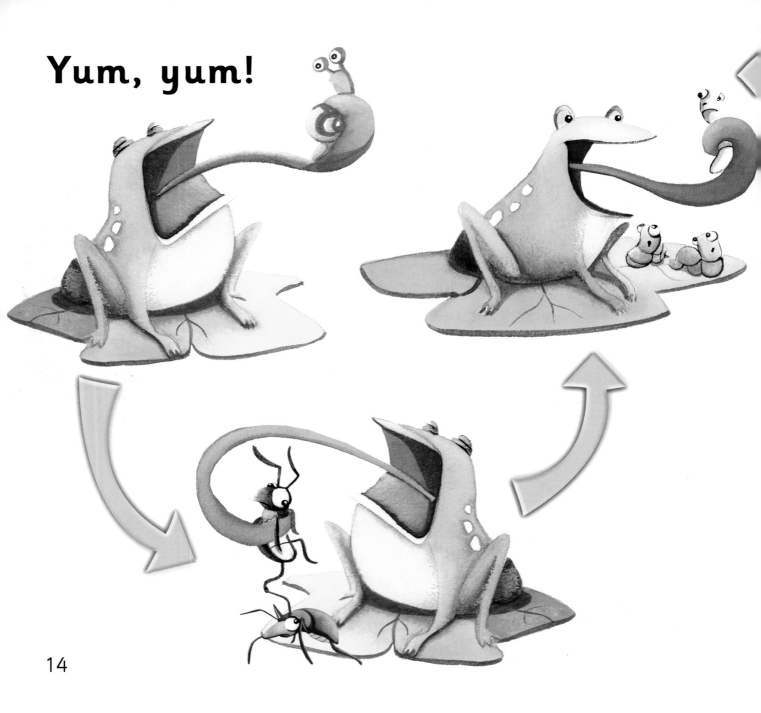

Ideas for reading

Written by Clare Dowdall BA(Ed), MA(Ed)
Lecturer and Primary Literacy Consultant

Learning objectives: retell narratives in the correct sequence, drawing on the language patterns of stories; use talk to organise, sequence and clarify thinking, ideas, feelings and events; use language to imagine and recreate roles and experiences; extend their vocabulary, exploring the meanings and sounds of new words

Curriculum links: Knowledge and Understanding of the World: Exploration and investigation

Interest words: snails, beetles, worms, spiders, flies, frogs

Word count: 18

Resources: whiteboard

Getting started

- Ask children to tell the group what they think frogs like to eat. Make a list of some ideas on a whiteboard.

- Look at the front and back covers together. Ask the children in pairs to read the title and the blurb, and to describe what is happening in the pictures.

- Ask children to share their ideas and to predict what is going to happen in the story.

Reading and responding

- Read pp2–3 together. Discuss the function of the dash and exclamation mark. Reread the words, modelling expressive reading.

- Introduce the term *speech bubble*. Explain that the frog is thinking aloud.

- Ask children to read the story independently and aloud to the end.

- Support children as they read, moving around the group and intervening where necessary to praise, encourage and help.

- Turn to p11 and focus on the shape in the water. Ask children to identify what it is and predict what will happen to the frog, then read pp12–13 together to see if they were correct.